THE TEAM

FRANCES MACKAY

Ransom

On the Ball
The Team
by Frances Mackay

Published by Ransom Publishing Ltd.
Radley House, 8 St. Cross Road, Winchester, Hampshire SO23 9HX, UK
www.ransom.co.uk

ISBN   978 178127 699 0
First published in 2014

Illustrated by Doreen Lang at GCI

THE TEAM

FRANCES MACKAY

The third book in the series
ON THE BALL

Ben and Matt were on their way to football practice.

'Mr Jones is going to tell us if we have enough money to buy the school football strip,' said Matt.

'We made a lot with our goal shoot,' said Ben. 'Let's hope everyone else did, too.'

The boys arrived just as Mr Jones was getting the footballs and cones from the PE cupboard.

'Hi, Mr Jones. Do you have good news to tell us?' asked Matt.

'Hello boys. I'm going to let you all know after practice. Come on, give me a hand with these,' said Mr Jones.

They walked to the playing field, where everyone else was waiting.

Mr Jones made sure everyone was warmed up first.

They did twenty star jumps and twenty windmills.

They jogged on the spot for five minutes.

Then they had to run around the field.

'Today I want to do some new skill work,' said Mr Jones.

The first skill game was called *Bull's-eye*.

Mr Jones split everyone into four teams.

Each team had four balls each.

Everyone in the team took turns to chip the balls into a circle with a cone in the centre.

The aim was to hit the cone, or 'bull's-eye'.

The bull's-eye had to be hit while keeping the ball moving.

It was a very fast game and it was hard to run and take careful aim at the same time.

Matt's team won the first game.

Matt hit the cone three times.

Dan was best. He hit the bull's-eye four times.

'OK, now I want you to do some dribbling practice,' said Mr Jones. 'I've made four squares with the cones. I want you to dribble the ball into the centre of the first square, then turn and dribble to each of the other squares. I will time each person.'

While everyone waited their turn, they played 'Keepy-Uppys' to see how long they could keep the ball in the air.

'Right, now we'll play a six-a-side game,' said
Mr Jones. 'I will be watching carefully to see who
will be picked for the team, so make sure you try
your best.'

For the first half, Ben and Matt played on the same side.

Ben was playing up front and he got the ball early in the
game.

As he raced off down the wing, he could see Matt up ahead to
his left.

He beat off a defender and passed the ball safely to Matt.

Matt raced ahead and took a shot at goal. It sailed through the air and hit the net.

'Yes!' yelled Matt, punching the air with his fist.

Dan was on the other team and he quickly got control of the ball.

Ben had to run hard to keep up with him.

'Dan, Dan, over here!' yelled Chris.

Dan looked across at Chris and slowed down for a moment.

It was just long enough for Ben to take the ball from him.

'Excellent!' thought Ben, as he raced away. 'I hope Matt's there for me.'

Sure enough, Matt was well placed again to take a shot.

Ben passed the ball and Matt took aim.

But this time the keeper was ready.

He dived far away to his right, just touching the ball and sending it over the bar.

'Nice try, Matt!' yelled Ben, as he raced back upfield.

Sim was playing really well.

She made a great tackle and got the ball.

She raced upfield and found Chris waiting for her.

She made an excellent pass and Chris was able to score.

The scores were even.

Tom was having a good game as keeper.

He kept his eye on the ball and worked really hard to stop each try.

He saved two more shots from Chris' team.

Mr Jones seemed to be watching him very carefully.

'Well done, Tom,' he shouted, when Tom saved the last shot.

Mr Jones blew the whistle and the game came to a stop.

Everyone looked very hot and tired.

'OK, that's enough for now,' said Mr Jones. 'Great game, well done everyone.'

'I wonder who will get in the team?' said Ben. 'There's twenty of us and only eleven and two subs will make it.'

'We both tried our best,' said Matt.

They all went into the classroom.

'Thanks for a great practice, everyone. I am going to have a very hard time picking the team for our first match. But as we play eight matches altogether, most of you should get a turn,' said Mr Jones. 'I will be telling you the team next week.'

Mr Jones then went on to talk about the fund-raising.

'You'll be very happy to learn that through all your hard work, we *will* have enough money to buy our new football strip,' he said.

'Yes!' everyone shouted.

'I'm picking the strip up tonight,' said Mr Jones. 'So you'll all be able to see it next week.'

Ben and Matt walked home together.

'It's like a dream come true,' said Ben. 'Our own school team *and* a new strip. I can't wait for next week.'

'Me neither,' said Matt.

But Ben and Matt didn't have to wait until next practice before they heard some news.

The very next day Mr Jones spoke to the whole school.

'I have some bad news to tell you,' he said. 'I had the new football strip in my car last night and it was stolen. Someone broke the back window and stole the whole lot.'

Ben looked at Matt.

Everyone became very quiet.

Mrs Hall, the Head Teacher, spoke next.

'I know how very hard the footballers have worked to earn the money for the strip. Mr Jones has worked hard to get the school league going. I am very shocked by this, as you are. We will try to think of a way to get another kit,' she said.

Ben and Matt walked home very slowly that afternoon.

It seemed like their dream had gone.

'Who would do such a thing?' asked Matt.

'Don't know,' said Ben. 'But I'd like to find out! All our hard work for nothing.'

Ben was very glum when he got home.

'What's the matter, love?' asked his mum.

Ben told her, and she became very upset.

'How dare they steal from little kids. What's the world coming to?' she said.

Later that night, Ben could hear his mum talking on the phone.

She spoke for a long time in a very quiet voice.

Ben wondered who she was talking to.

He felt really angry about the stolen strip.

'It's not fair,' he said. 'It's just not fair!'

The next week, after practice, Mr Jones called them all together.

'We don't have an answer to our football strip problem. But I do have an idea and I hope to let you know more next week,' he said.

Ben raised his eyebrows and looked across at Matt.

'I wonder what Mr Jones is going to do?' he said.

'And now for the important bit,' said Mr Jones. 'I've picked the team for our first match against Brent Park Primary.'

Ben held his breath.

He wanted to be in the team more than anything.

He couldn't bear to look at Mr Jones' face as he read out the team.

He closed his eyes and crossed his fingers.

'Dan, Chris, David and Sim. You will play in midfield.'

Ben opened his eyes.

Only seven more people to go.

'Joe, Sara, Jack and Oliver will play at the back, as defenders.'

Ben held his breath again.

Three more to go.

'Tom, I'd like you to be keeper.'

Only two more people to go.

'And Ben and Matt. I want you two to play up front as forwards.'

Ben let out his breath with a deep sigh.

He felt so happy he could hardly believe it.

At last all his hard work had paid off — he was in the team.

'The two subs will be Ramjeet and Paul.

'Well done those who made the team. If you didn't make it this time, there's always the next match. I want you all to keep training hard — after all, we do want to win, don't we?'

Ben and Matt walked home together again.

'We did it!' said Matt, slapping Ben on the back.

'Yes. I can't wait to beat the socks off Brent Park. I just wish we had a school strip. I want us to look like a proper team,' said Ben.

'Yeah, me too,' said Matt. 'Do you think Mr Jones will come up with a new strip in time?'

'I hope so,' said Ben. 'I really hope so.'

The next book in the series is:

MATT

HOW MANY HAVE YOU READ?